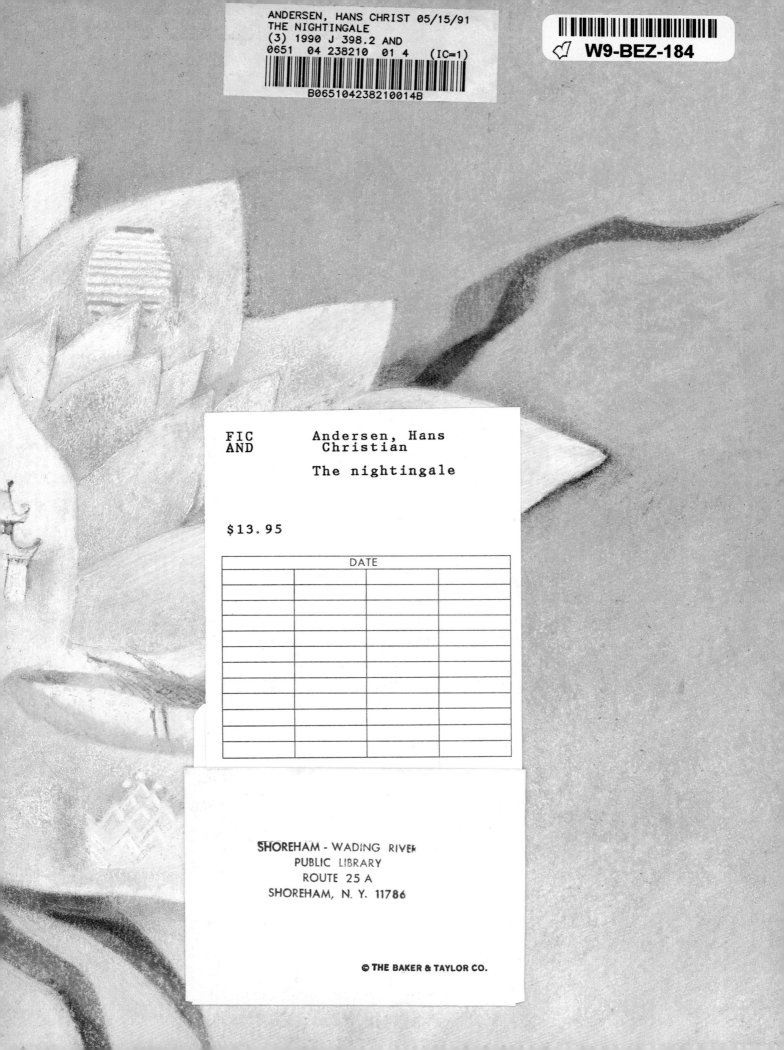

DATE			

The Nightingale

Hans Christian Andersen
The Nightingale

Translated and with an Introduction by

Naomi Lewis

Illustrated by

Josef Paleček

North-South Books
New York

Introduction

When you start to read *The Nightingale* you know that you have stepped into a proper fairy tale: a wondrous palace, a garden that runs on and on, so far that no one knows where it ends, a forest (of course) whose furthest trees overhang the deep blue waters of the sea. And somewhere within all this a marvel of marvels—or so they say. There's comedy too; you have to smile at those ridiculous courtiers in the wood. But read a few pages more—the story is quite short—and you know that this is a very great fairy tale, one that only Andersen could have written. There are passages in his stories that stay in your mind forever. Kay's flight through the midnight sky in the Snow Queen's sledge is one. Elisa's ride through the clouds with her wild swan brothers is another. A third, absolutely, is the great scene in *The Nightingale* where the bird wins the Emperor's life from Death.

How did these ideas come into Andersen's head? We need to go back to his own beginnings, as one of the poorest boys in the Danish town of Odense, where he was born in 1805. His life was indeed like a fairy tale; but with very grim fairy-tale hardships and trials before the triumphant end. His mother was a washerwoman, his father a shoemaker—not a good one either, but in those days he had no choice in the matter of work. This father was clever in other ways though. He studied and read when he could and had ideas of his own on religion and politics (which alarmed the simple, pious mother). He made his boy a beautiful toy theatre and on Sundays would take him into the woods and fields and show him how every insect, flower and blade of grass had a life and character of its own. This would be the basis of so many of Andersen's stories; all human situations seen through *things* or (as in *Thumbelina*) on a tiny scale.

But the father died when Hans Christian was eleven. If only he could have known that the boy, whom the villagers thought half crazy, would, as a man, be honored all over the world, and remain so, wherever books are read and stories told.

But this did not happen yet. At fourteen young Andersen set off for Copenhagen—a lanky scarecrow with hair the color of straw, hoping to make a living by singing, dancing and clowning. What was to be done with this young troll, this odd, determined childlike creature, always knocking at famous people's doors? A fund was collected and he was sent off to be educated. School was horrible; he was starved and ill-treated by the headmaster, at whose house he lodged, and tormented by the boys, all younger and smaller than himself. But he persevered and at last was free to choose what to do in life. He became a writer, at first of grown-up novels and plays. But it was the little tales that he also wrote that began to make his name. They were so original, like nothing else in print!

Now that he had found his gift, ideas came to Andersen from everywhere—from things in the room where he was sitting, the chairs, the crockery, from the woods and streets, a broken toy in the gutter, from earliest memories. And *The Nightingale*? In his own account of his life he tells this childhood story:

An old woman washing out clothes in the Odense river told me that the Empire of China lay directly underneath. I did not think it impossible that a Chinese prince, on some moonlit night, might dig himself up through the earth, hearing me sing. He would take me down to his kingdom, make me rich and noble, and then let me return to Odense. There I would live in style and build myself a castle. I spent many an evening working out the plans for this.

Readers who like to play the detective game might note that, in one guise or another, sometimes just for a fleeting moment, Andersen himself may be found in most of his stories. Sometimes he briefly appears as a poor student or poet; at the end of *Thumbelina* he is "the man who tells fairy tales." If someone in a tale is cutting out paper dolls and castles you may be sure who *that* is. Paper cutting was one of Andersen's quite remarkable skills. *The Ugly Duckling* is his own tale throughout; he was indeed the misfit who became a swan.

And what is he in *The Nightingale*? There is a little of him, maybe, in the fisherman and the kitchen maid; but really, I suspect, he is the nightingale itself, a bird without possessions except a marvelous voice (for Andersen, that means his storytelling); a bird that sees many things, good and bad, joyful and sad, and puts them into its songs. "I shall bring you happiness but also serious thoughts," the bird says to the Emperor. That is just what Andersen does, so lightly and so magically, in the story we have here.

Naomi Lewis

$\mathbf{Y}$OU KNOW, OF COURSE, that in China the Emperor is Chinese, and so are all the people around him. This story happened many a year ago, but that's exactly why you should hear it now, before it is forgotten.

The Emperor's palace was the most marvelous in the world. It was made all through of the finest porcelain; you had to take the greatest care when you moved about. The palace garden—that was a wonder too. It was full of exquisite flowers, never seen anywhere else. The loveliest of all had little silver bells tied to them—tinkle, tinkle, tinkle—to make sure that no one passed without noticing.

Yes, it was a wonderful garden—and it stretched so far that even the gardener had no idea where it ended.

If you kept on walking, you would find yourself at last in a beautiful forest, with towering trees and deep, still lakes. This forest went right down to the sea which was the bluest of blues, and so deep that great ships could sail by under the high branches of the trees.

In these branches lived a nightingale.

She sang so sweetly that even the poor fisherman would forget his cares for a moment and stop to listen. "Ah, it's a treat to hear it," he would say. But then he would have to get on with his work, and put the bird out of his mind. Yet the very next night, and the next, as soon as the nightingale sang again, he would look up and say once more, "Ah, it's a treat to hear it."

From every country in the world, travelers came to admire the Emperor's palace and his garden. But as soon as they heard the nightingale sing, they would declare, "Now, *that's* the best thing of all."

When they were back at home, these travelers still went on talking about the bird. Learned men wrote books about the palace and the garden, but they praised one marvel more than all the rest, and this was the nightingale. These books were read by people everywhere in the world, and one day they reached the Emperor himself.

There he sat in his golden chair, reading and reading, now and then nodding his head, for he was pleased. Then he came to the sentence "But the greatest of all these wonders is the nightingale."

"The nightingale?" said the Emperor. "What is that? I've never heard of it. What strange things one learns from books!" And he sent for his High Chief Lord-in-Waiting.

"I see in this book," he said, "that we have a remarkable bird called the nightingale. It's supposed to be the finest thing in my empire. Why has no one ever told me about it? It's a disgrace that the whole world knows what I possess—and I don't. You must arrange for the bird to come here tonight and sing for me."

"I have never heard anyone mention the bird," said the High Chief Lord-in-Waiting. "But I'll investigate. I'll find it."

Yes, but how and where? Up and down the great stairs he went, in and out of rooms and passages, but not a single person had ever heard of the nightingale.

"It must be an invented tale, Your Imperial Majesty," he told the Emperor.

But the Emperor was determined to hear the bird, that very night. So the High Chief Lord-in-Waiting set off running again, and now, half the court ran with him.

At last they reached the kitchen, and there they found a poor little kitchen maid. "The nightingale?" she said. "My goodness, yes, of course I know her. Most evenings they let me take some scraps to my sick mother. She lives by the lake at the other side of the forest. When I am tired I sit down to rest, and then I hear the nightingale."

"Little kitchen maid," said the Lord-in-Waiting. "I can guarantee you a permanent kitchen appointment if you will lead us to the bird. But it has to appear at the palace this very evening. We must start now."

So they set out for the forest, and half the court trailed along with them. A cow began to moo. "Oh, there it is," said a page. "I rather fancy I've heard that sound before. But what a big noise for something as small as a bird."

"No—that's just a cow mooing," said the little girl. "We've a long way to go yet."

Some frogs began to croak. "Ah, there it is!" said the palace chaplain. "What a glorious sound! Just like tiny church bells!"

"No, those are frogs," said the little kitchen maid. "But I think we'll hear her any minute now."

Then the nightingale began to sing. "There she is!" said the girl. "Look!" And she pointed to a little gray bird in the branches.

"Is it possible?" said the Lord-in-Waiting. "The creature looks so ordinary. Perhaps the sight of all these distinguished people has made it lose its color."

"Little nightingale!" said the kitchen maid. "Our gracious Emperor would very much like you to sing for him."

"With the greatest pleasure," said the nightingale, and she sang so beautifully that it was a delight to hear.

"It sounds just like glass bells," said the Lord-in-Waiting. "I can't imagine why we have never heard it before. It will be a sensation at court!"

"Shall I sing once again for the Emperor?" asked the nightingale. She thought that the Emperor was one of these visitors.

"Most excellent nightingale!" said the Lord-in-Waiting. "I have the honor to summon you to a concert this evening at the palace, where you will enchant His Imperial Majesty with your elegant song."

"It sounds best in the green forest," said the nightingale. Still, she went along willingly enough when she heard that the Emperor wished it.

Meanwhile, what a cleaning and polishing was going on at the palace. The porcelain walls and floor shone and sparkled in the light of thousands of golden lamps. Right in the middle of the great hall, before the Emperor's throne, a golden perch was set up; this was for the nightingale. Everyone in the court was there, even the little kitchen maid. She was allowed to stand behind the door, for she now had the official title Genuine Maid of the Kitchen. And now, all eyes were turned on the little gray bird, as the Emperor nodded at her to begin.

Then the nightingale sang so beautifully that the Emperor's eyes filled with tears which rolled right down his cheeks. The bird sang on, even more thrillingly, and every note went straight to the Emperor's heart.

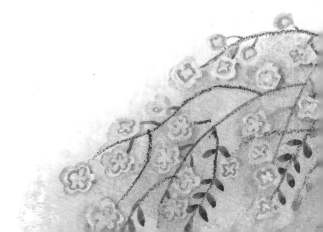

The Emperor now declared that the nightingale should have his own golden slipper to wear round her neck. But she thanked him, saying that she could not accept the gift. "I have seen the tears in the Emperor's eyes—can any reward be greater than that? An emperor's tears have a rare power. They are reward enough." And then she sang yet another song in her ravishing voice.

She was a great success; no doubt about that. And now she was to remain at court, in a special cage, with permission to take the air twice in the daytime and once at night. On each of these outings she was to be accompanied by twelve attendants, each one holding firmly on to a silk ribbon tied to the bird's leg. No—these excursions were not much fun!

One day, a large parcel arrived for the Emperor. On it was written a single word: NIGHTINGALE.

"Why, here's a new book about our famous bird!" said the Emperor. But it was not a book; it was a little mechanical toy in a box, a clockwork nightingale. It was made to look like the real one, but it was covered all over with diamonds, rubies and sapphires. If you wound it up it would sing one of the songs that the real bird sang, and its tail would go up and down, glittering with silver and gold. Round its neck hung a ribbon, embroidered with these words: THE EMPEROR OF JAPAN'S NIGHTINGALE IS A POOR THING BESIDE THE NIGHTINGALE OF THE EMPEROR OF CHINA.

The messenger who had brought the bird from the Emperor of Japan was given the title Chief Imperial Bringer of Nightingales. And it was decided that the two birds should sing together. "What a duet that will be!" said the courtiers.

But the duet was not a success. The trouble was that the real nightingale sang in her own way, and the other bird's song came out of a machine.

So the clockwork bird was set to sing alone. It pleased the court quite as much as the real one—and, of course, it was a great deal prettier to look at, sparkling away like a bracelet or a brooch. Over and over, thirty-three times, it sang the same tune, and yet it was not in the least tired. The courtiers would gladly have heard it a few times more, but now the Emperor thought that the real one should have a turn.

But—where *was* the nightingale?

Where was she? She had flown out of the open window, away to her own green forest, and no one had noticed.

"Tut, tut, tut!" said the Emperor. " What's the meaning of this?" The courtiers said "Tut, tut" too, and frowned. "Still, we have the better bird here," they added, and asked to hear the clockwork bird again. This was the thirty-fourth time. Then the Master of the Imperial Music praised the clockwork bird in the highest terms. "You see, Your Imperial Majesty, with the real nightingale you can never tell what will happen, but with the clockwork bird, everything is clear. You can open it and see how it works, how each note must precisely follow the one before."

"Why, that's just what I was thinking," said one courtier to another. And the following Sunday the Master of the Imperial Music was allowed to give a public display of the bird to the ordinary people. "They too must hear it sing," the Emperor declared. And hear it they did: it made them feel light-headed. They all said, "Ah-h-h!" and nodded their heads, and held their forefingers up in the air to show how much they appreciated the bird.

But the poor fisherman who had heard the real nightingale said, "It's pretty enough. Yet there's something missing. I don't know what."

The real nightingale was banished from the Emperor's realm.

The artificial bird was awarded a special place on a silk cushion close to the Emperor's bed—piled around were all the gifts it had been given, all the gold and jewels. It was honored with the title High Imperial Minstrel of the Bedside Table, Class One.

A whole year passed. The Emperor, his court and his people now knew by heart every trill in the toy bird's song—but they liked it all the more for that. They could join in the song themselves, and this they did.

But one evening, just as the bird was singing away, and the Emperor was lying in bed listening to it, something went "Crack!". Then "Whirr-rr-rr". The wheels went whizzing round and the music stopped. The Emperor leapt out of bed and sent for his doctor. But what was the use of that? So they went and fetched the watchmaker, and he managed to patch up the bird after a fashion. But he warned them that it would have to be used very sparingly. The bearings were almost worn away and could not be replaced.

That was a dreadful blow! They dared not let the bird sing more than once a year, and that was taking a risk.

Five years passed, and a great sorrow fell upon the land. The Emperor was gravely ill and was not expected to live. Crowds stood outside in the street and asked for news. Each time the Lord-in-Waiting shook his head.

Cold and pale the Emperor lay in his royal bed. Indeed, the whole court now believed him gone, and went running off to greet his successor. But the Emperor was not dead. There he lay, pale and unmoving, in his magnificent bed with its long velvet curtains and heavy tassels of gold. Through a high open window the moon shone down on the Emperor and the clockwork bird.

The poor Emperor could hardly breathe; he felt as if something were sitting on his heart. He opened his eyes. Yes, Death was seated there. Death was wearing on his head the Emperor's golden crown. And, out of the folds of the great velvet curtains, the strangest faces pushed and peeped. Some were hideous; some were lovely and kind. They were the Emperor's evil and good deeds, and they all stared back at him. "Do you remember...?" "Do you remember...?" Their rustling whispers went on, one after another. And they told so many things that the sweat broke out on the Emperor's forehead.

"Music! Music!" he cried. "Beat the great drum of China! Save me from these voices!"

But the voices did not stop. And Death nodded like a mandarin at everything that was said.

"Oh, let me have music!" begged the Emperor. "Beautiful little golden bird, sing! I have given you gold and precious gifts. Sing, I beseech you, sing!"

But the bird was silent. There was no one to wind it up. Everything was still, terribly still.

Then, all at once, close by the window, the loveliest song rang out. It came from the living nightingale. She had heard of the Emperor's need and had flown back to bring him comfort and hope. As she sang, the ghostly forms grew more and more shadowy, and thinned away into nothing. A living warmth began to flow through the Emperor's body. Death himself was enchanted by the song. "Sing more—sing more, little nightingale," said Death.

"Yes, if you will give me the Emperor's crown."

And Death gave up the treasure in return for a song, and the nightingale went on singing. She sang of the quiet churchyard where the white roses grow, where the elder flowers smell so sweetly, where the fresh grass is kept green by the tears of those who mourn. Then Death was filled with a great longing for his garden, and he floated out of the window like a cold white mist.

"Thank you, thank you," said the Emperor. "I banished you from my realm, yet you alone came to my aid and drove the dreadful phantoms from my bed; you freed my heart from Death. How can I reward you?"

"You *have* rewarded me," said the nightingale. "When I first sang for you, tears came into your eyes, and that gift I cannot forget. Those are jewels that cannot be bought or sold. But now you must sleep. Listen, I will sing to you."

She sang, and the Emperor fell into a deep refreshing sleep.

When he awoke, the sun was shining through the window. All his illness, all his weakness were gone, but the nightingale was still there.

"You must stay with me always," said the Emperor. "You need sing only when you wish. As for the clockwork bird, I'll break it into a thousand pieces."

"Don't do that," said the nightingale. "It has done what it could for you. For my part, I can't make my home in a palace, but let me come and go as I wish; then, in the evenings, I'll sit on the branch by the window and sing for you. I shall bring you happiness but also serious thoughts. I shall sing of the good and the evil that are all around you and yet have always been hidden from you. The little bird flies far and wide, to the poor fisherman and the laborer's cottage, to people far away from your splendid court. I love your heart more than your crown—yet the crown has some magic about it. Yes, I will come, but there is one thing you must promise."

"Anything," said the Emperor. He had risen and put on his imperial robes.

"This is the thing I ask you. Tell no one that you have a little bird for a friend who gives you all the news. Just keep it a secret." With that, she flew away.

The servants came in to look after their dead master. Well—there they stood!

"Good morning!" said the Emperor.

This text was translated from
the original story, *Nattergalen*, published in 1844.

Copyright © 1990 by Nord-Süd Verlag AG, Gossau Zürich, Switzerland
First published in Switzerland under the title *Die Nachtigall*
English translation copyright © 1990 by Naomi Lewis

First published in the United States, Great Britain, Canada,
Australia and New Zealand in 1990 by North-South Books,
an imprint of Nord-Süd Verlag AG, Gossau Zürich, Switzerland.

Library of Congress Catalog Card Number: 89-43723
ISBN 1-55858-090-5
British Library Cataloguing in Publication Data is available.

1 3 5 7 9 10 8 6 4 2

Printed in Belgium